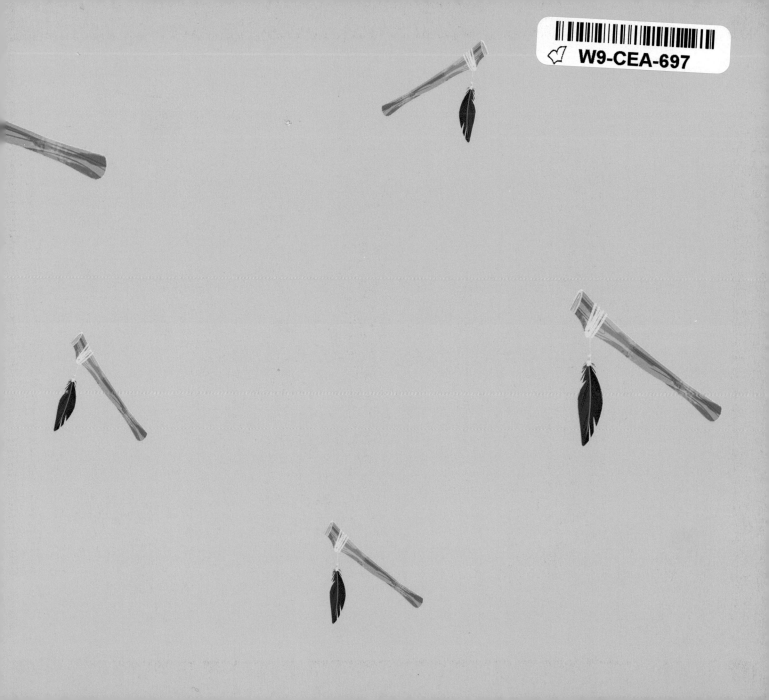

Dedication:
This book is dedicated with love to my husband Lynn and to our son River, and to
ALL the rivers that carry life to the lands. This book is also dedicated, with big love and
thanks, to the amazing Teddy, Emma and Jessika — folks at Medicine Wheel Education.
They are a perfect circle of talent.

Editor: Allison Parker and Emma Bullen
Text and illustration copyright © Medicine Wheel Education Inc. 2019
ISBN: 978-1-9891222-3-5
For more book information, visit www.medicinewheel.education

The Circle of Caring and Sharing is an adaptation of the beautiful book **The Sharing Circle**, by Corky Larsen-Jonasson, for a younger audience (ages 4-6). In order to connect with this age group, the story has been simplified and given a rhyming scheme. This book was made with Corky and has her enthusiastic approval. We are excited for you to read it and hope that you enjoy it!

There once were two foxes who were best friends,
and they lived on the plains where the sky never ends.

One day, these two foxes had a terrible fight,
and were no longer friends when they went home that night.

The two foxes refused to talk the next day,
which made their friends sad and not want to play.

An older buffalo knew just what to do,
she went to Kokom the owl who said
"who-who who!"

"We should hold a sharing circle today,
so that we can all hear what our friends have to say."

So they gathered the animals from all around
to come sit in a circle on the ground.
"This circle is sacred,
this circle's for sharing
and connects the community
in a way that is caring."

We're gathered today because of a fight,
to bring all our feelings out into the light.

The animals took turns passing the stick to speak.
Some gave a loud roar, and others a squeak.

The foxes listened to each other explain
why their feelings were hurt and causing them pain.

Now that the foxes understood what went wrong,
they could go back to getting along.

The animals thanked Kokom for bringing them together.
They knew they would be friends forever and ever.

Plains Cree Animals and Their Phonetic Pronunciations:

Owl = Oohoo (oo-hoo)

Skunk = Sikak (si-gawk)

Fox = Mahkesis (muck-sees)

Rabbit = Wapos (wah poose)

Prairie chicken = Ahkisew (ahh-ki-sew)

Buffalo = Puskwa Moostos (pus-kwah moos-toes)

About the Author:

Theresa "Corky" Larsen-Jonasson is a respected elder, as identified by her community, with roots in Red Deer, Didsbury and Maskwacis First Nations. She lives her life according to the traditional Indigenous teachings that saved her life. These teachings flow from her parents, her Kokom, Christine Joseph of Cochrane, aunties, uncles, as well as from the Goodstrikers, Williams and John Crier families, all of whom she loves immensely. Corky serves as a member of the national Walking With Our Sisters collective as a part of the missing and murdered Indigenous women awareness movement, and a proud member of Red Deer's Red Feather Women. She is also a member of the Urban Aboriginal Voices Women's Council and the Red Deer Welcoming and Inclusive Communities Network.

MEDICINE WHEEL EDUCATION

MEDICINE WHEEL EDUCATION

www.medicinewheel.education

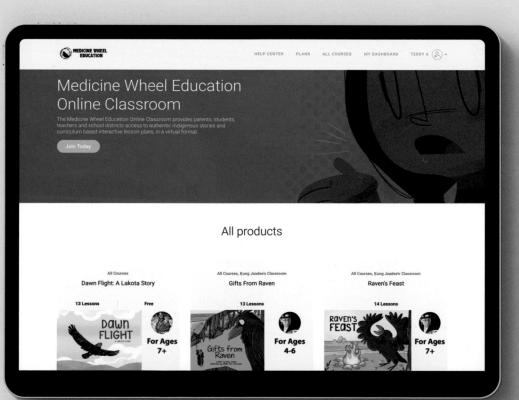

Online Courses Available:
www.classroom.medicinewheel.education